Toestomper and the Bad Butterflies

To my grandchildren, Laura and Alexandre,
and their wonderful parents, Eric and Sylvie Pederson.

All rights reserved. For information about permission to reproduce
selections from this book, write to Permissions, Houghton Mifflin
Company, 215 Park Avenue South, New York, New York 10003.

www.houghtonmifflinbooks.com

The text of this book is set in 16-point Cremona.
The illustrations are gouache, reproduced in full color.

Library of Congress Cataloging-in-Publication Data
Collicott, Sharleen.
Toestomper and the bad butterflies / written and illustrated by Sharleen Collicott.
p. cm.
Summary: Toestomper doesn't mind having baby caterpillars invade his
home because they make such nice pets, but when they change
into butterflies and begin zooming around Littletown, no one is safe.
ISBN 0-618-14092-1
[1. Caterpillars—Fiction. 2. Butterflies—Fiction. 3. Pets—Fiction.
4. Behavior—Fiction. 5. Daredevils—Fiction.] I. Title.
PZ7.C67758 Tl 2003   [Fic]—dc21   2002000475

Printed in Singapore
TWP 10 9 8 7 6 5 4 3 2 1

Toestomper and the Bad Butterflies

Sharleen Collicott

Houghton Mifflin Company

Boston 2003

Toestomper lived in a hut outside Littletown. Ever since the baby caterpillars moved in, he had been very busy. Toestomper didn't mind. He liked the caterpillars.

In the mornings, he took his caterpillars for long walks. "Stay close, my blue fuzzies," Toestomper told them, "or you might get lost."

Every afternoon, his caterpillars played outside.
If the iguanas came near, Toestomper shouted, "Get away,
you scaly monsters!"

At night, when it thundered, Toestomper let the caterpillars
sleep in his bed.

Life went on like this until . . .

...one day, the caterpillars completely covered themselves with strange blankets, went to sleep, and wouldn't wake up.

Toestomper stomped and yelled, "Get up, you lazy lie-abouts." But the caterpillars kept sleeping.

Toestomper went to Littletown and asked the doctor what to do. "Let them sleep," the doctor advised. "They're tired."

After several lonely weeks, Toestomper saw the blankets wiggle, and out crawled sleepy butterflies. "Who are you?" Toestomper demanded.

"We used to be your caterpillars," the butterflies explained. "Now we're your butterflies."

Toestomper watched in amazement as his new butterflies yawned and unfolded their wings. Soon they were zigzagging around the room.

The wobbly butterflies bumped into a lamp and knocked over dishes.

"Careful!" Toestomper cried. "You're going to get hurt."

Outside, the butterflies fluttered back and forth.
"Fly higher," Toestomper urged. "You'll be safer up there."

"This is as high as we can go," the butterflies explained.

"Nonsense," Toestomper said. "If you can fly low, you can
fly high."

Toestomper took his butterflies to the pond, where the
frogs lived.
"See how high the frogs can jump?" he said. "You'll have
to fly higher than that, or the frogs will eat you for lunch."

"That's too high for us," the butterflies complained.

"No it's not, you scaredy-cats," Toestomper growled.
"Just flap your wings faster."

Suddenly, a frog stuck his head out of the water.
The butterflies scattered in all directions.

"You low-flying flappers have to learn go higher,"
Toestomper explained.
"Then, nothing can get you, not even Big Tooth!"

"Big Tooth?" the butterflies said. "Who's that?"

"He's the biggest giant of all," Toestomper answered
as he picked up his butterflies and climbed into a tree.

Toestomper climbed to the top and put the butterflies on a branch.
"Now, fly!" he ordered.

The butterflies hung on tight and closed their eyes.
"We're afraid," they cried.

Toestomper ripped off some small branches and wove them together.
Then he jumped off the tree, holding on to his rickety wings!

"This is fun!" Toestomper called to the butterflies. "See? There's nothing to be afraid of."

The butterflies opened their eyes to watch. "Those are dumb wings," they said. "They only go down. Flap faster and you'll go up."

"Show me," Toestomper yelled as he started to fall.

The butterflies flew off the branch and soared up into the air as Toestomper crashed to the ground.

"We have better wings than you," the butterflies bragged.

Soon the butterflies were zooming back and forth and doing loop-di-loops. They streaked close to the pond, just to let the frogs know they were no longer afraid.

Toestomper had taught his butterflies too well. Now that they felt so brave, the butterflies did exactly as they pleased.

They zoomed the iguanas. "You used to scare us, but not anymore!" the butterflies yelled.

They even started causing trouble in town.
"Toestomper, get your bad butterflies out of here,"
the townsfolk cried.

The butterflies were completely out of control.
Toestomper started to worry.

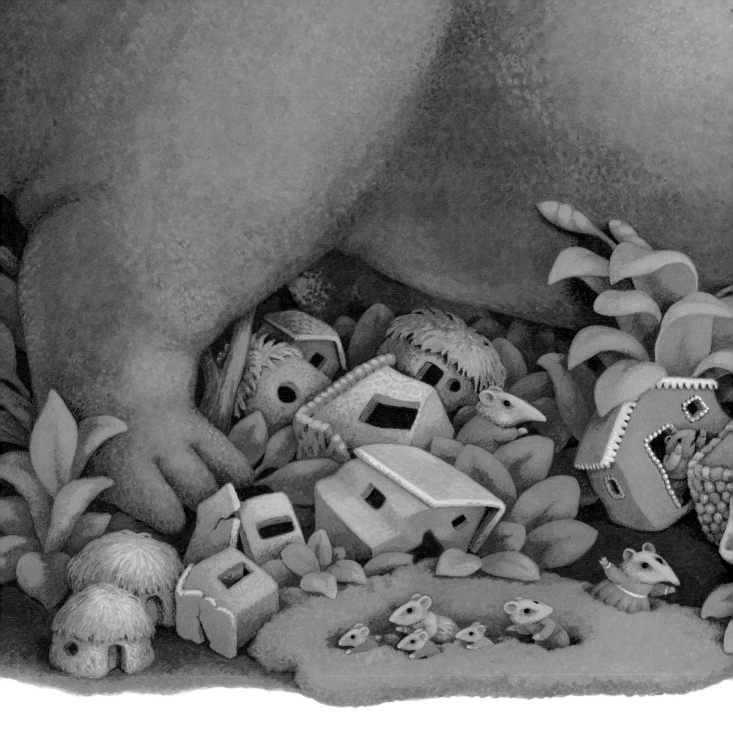

But soon the townsfolk forgot about the butterflies because
the ground shook, and Big Tooth came smashing into town.

The townsfolk ran out of their homes.
"The giant is here!" they yelled. "Run for your lives!"

After eating a few bushes, Big Tooth yawned. He was ready
for a nap.

"Look out!" the frantic townsfolk cried. "Big Tooth is going to
sleep on our houses."

Toestomper ran to town to see what all the commotion was about. His butterflies flew ahead.

When Toestomper saw the giant, he yelled to his butterflies, "Fly high, where it's safe."

"We're not afraid of Big Tooth!" the butterflies bragged. "We're going to zoom him."

"Don't do it, you crazy daredevils!" Toestomper shouted. "That giant is too big!"

Big Tooth snuggled down in the center of town, right on top of the houses, and closed his eyes.

"He's sleeping," the butterflies said. "Let's tickle his ears." And down they dove, straight at Big Tooth's ears.

Big Tooth leaped up and he was mad. He didn't like to be
bothered while sleeping. Big Tooth snapped and chomped
at the butterflies, catching them in his mouth.

Inside Big Tooth's mouth it was very dark. The butterflies were terrified and flew back and forth, bumping into the sides of Big Tooth's throat.

Big Tooth went *"kerchooooey, kerchooooey,"* sending the butterflies sailing out into the air. Then he galloped away, coughing and sneezing.

The townsfolk cheered and clapped. "Those butterflies are the bravest and the toughest," they said.

But the butterflies didn't feel so brave and tough. They knew what it was like to make Big Tooth mad, and to be almost swallowed.

Toestomper picked up his soggy, wilted butterflies.
He took them home, dried them off, and fed them dinner.

"You've been brave enough, my little gladiators," Toestomper said.
"From now on, I want you to act more like regular butterflies.
Maybe check out the flowers once in a while."

And that's what the butterflies did. Of course, they still zoomed, but only at ladybugs and tiny spiders.

And sometimes the butterflies bragged about how they had made Big Tooth run away and saved Littletown.

Luckily, Big Tooth never came back, and everyone was glad, especially the butterflies.